# MY FAVOURITE MERMAID ALEXA

KA. PARINASRI - MOHAMMED NIYAZ

*Mermaids are always my favourite!!*

*well, it wasn't from yesterday or a kinda recent addition,*
*They are my favourite from a young age!*

# Contents

# Acknowledgements

A human cum fish creature is up about to inspire you with multiple thoughts and purposes equally. It's your one chance take to manage the decisions of ur mindful tacts and turns. "**My Favourite Mermaid Alexa**" is a soulful book **compiled** by **KA. Parinasri** And **Mohammed Niyaz respectively.** We are thankful to the team of Notion Press for having immense faith in us to compile this beautiful anthology. We are also thankful to our "**14 co-authors**" for pouring out their wonderful thoughts under this book. We hope our readers have a great time out there with the same.

• • •

"**My Favourite Mermaid Alexa**" is a work of fiction. All the thoughts, writings has been penned by the imaginative purpose of the writers itself. We do not take any responsibilities in case of plagiarism of content found as the publication, founders nor the compilers would be responsible for this. The writers will be the sole source of the above same.

# Foreword

*An imaginary vision could be a chance which may reach chances to reinvent our purpose of thoughts. A creature which portrays the adventures through so many unbelievable mysteries yet untold. Behind those secrets you could be the only one who can come closure to the realisations of different soughts after. "**My Favourite Mermaid Alexa**" is a combination of mixed feelings penned by **a co-operative team of 14 co-authors,** we present you a variations of different genres as well taste of feelings hidden under the truth that lies beneath the minds and thoughts of the same.*

# Preface

## KA. PARINASRI

*(COMPILER)*

*KA. PARINASRI*

*She is a passionate writer from Chennai. Writing makes her pressure go away. She had played the role of co-author for more than 100+, Compiled 30+ Books, And she is compiling many more which is on progress!*

*Her 1st and foremost book as a compiler was 'MY PEN FLOWS MY PAPER RECEIVES'*

*Wish You Were My Better Half is one of her favourite anthology - which hit the award for compiling it within 24 hours.*

*Well, She would like to thank her Loved ones for supporting her rather than stopping her from what she wanted to do! For being the main reason for achieving her dream.*

*She believes that anyone could hurt her, But never her books could!!*

*She had published 2 solo books.*

1. *JP: The Blessed Better Half*
2. *The Utmost Desire of Roaring Shout*

*Her Dual books*

1. *The Ink They Shared Through Words*
2. *The Collaborate Authors*

*As well working on with her other solo and dual books!*

• • •

*Let's get into the story of KA. PARINASRI visited the Mermaid show and let's get to know whether as per her wish did she meet the mermaid in person and did she take at least a single picture with the Mermaid.*

*All of a sudden I happen to visit the Marine kingdom in Chennai N'th time.*

*I visited the Marine kingdom, I spent a few hours happily, Well I was about to leave the kingdom and almost came to the end of the place, all of a sudden mermaid thought crossed my mind, and I started in search of a mermaid,*

*Well whoever crossed my path, I started enquiring about the mermaid, As if in the feel of mermaids are regularly being in the kingdom,*

*Who knows mermaid shows are seasonal shows!*

*I wasn't even aware that the mermaid show is seasonal.*

*After which a person guided me to the management team, I took a step forward and enquired about Isn't the marine kingdom have mermaid?*

*They were like mam we invite the professional mermaid for the few mins of the show, and they are of the seasonal show,*

*And my next question was when would the show happen next?*

*They said mam maybe kinda starts from December happens until New year!*

*I was like damn I missed it, How would I get the information? Like if the show would happen in the month of may properly?*

*They were like give a call at the start of the month, we would inform you whether we are arranging for the show or not!*

*I was like okay. Thank you.*

*Well, let's meet in May!.*

*And the months passed and finally, May month started, well called up and asked them for the details, And they said we have 4 shows and the timing!*

*I already made sure am just visiting the marine kingdom Just for the mermaid show, as I visited the kingdom plenty of times within the few months!*

*So this time I took my family members and I was too much ever to visit the mermaid and was too crazy and exciting to take at least a single picture with her.*

*Well knowing the 4 scheduled timing for the mermaid show, We entered the Marine kingdom, Damn I have never seen this huge crowd at the ticket counter, The show already started and I was suffering to get the ticket with the huge line.*

*My heart was saying the show is gonna end up with getting the tickets fast and visiting the show.*

*Uff.. finally got rickets for your family and Stepped in The 1st question to the photographer was where is the Mermaid show going on?..*

*They replied at the end of this Marine kingdom,*

*So I rushed up and my family was running behind me well I visited plenty of times so I already know where it starts and ends, Whereas my family is visiting for the 1st time and they also came with the eagerness of visiting the mermaid.*

*Well, the sad part was I went to the end of the kingdom and found that the show had just ended, with the disappointment sat down there for a few minutes, I wasn't aware that on weekends they had th different schedule for the same show.*

*Felt too disappointed, it as well felt like I wasted the 4000 Rupees. And then My father went to the management team to enquire about when is the next show?*

*On the other side, my Brother went and asked few staff who were standing near the escalator.*

*And other were sitting beside me and was trying to console me saying don't worry dear, what if we miss this show, we will wait until the next show and meet her!*

*Well am the adamant kid, it isn't that easy to calm me.*

*I was fully disappointed and I was just troubling everyone and we were just walking up and down,*

*Just in search of the mermaid,*

*I didn't ever allow anyone to visit anyone of the variety of fishes or cave or anything which were was in the marine kingdom, I didn't ever allow anyone to take even a single picture peacefully Because I already visited plenty of times so I already know what's all there,*

*All I want to visit is the mermaid and her just 10 minutes show. Nothing felt too surprising to me.*

*Well after 3 hours I heard the announcement of the mermaid show, So I told my family members and I ran to get to know about the announcement and my family were being behind me, So heard she would be on all the 5 screens, So we took the place on the 3rd screen and sat on the front of the mirror so that we would be able to see her nearby,*

*Well, I was expecting for the bubble heart, But she didn't give the bubble heart at all, only while entering she gave, But I was glad because saw her nearby.*

*Well even over her I didn't allow my mom to watch the show peacefully, Because I assigned the work of taking videos and pictures.*

*Well, even though when the mermaid came nearby I was happily watching her and was seeing the way she was moving the mermaid style, but were as I didn't allow my mom to enjoy watching the show, Even though the mermaid came to mean by, I didn't allow my mom to see her peacefully, Because she was focusing on taking video of the mermaid and I was giving poses to taking pictures,*

*I may wait but the mermaid wouldn't wait for me na, The mermaid would swim and move on!*

*Well being the biggest spoiler to my family, I wasn't peaceful and didn't allow my family to have a peaceful time.*

*I use to follow many, well-known famous mermaids, Who are Instagram accounts are even certified, Well those are famous ones too, But yet I had the feeling of I couldn't visit them in reality with the mermaid getup.*

*I use to check their reels, where they swim in the sea with the mermaid dress, and a few use to do shows, well I was also jealous of the people who use to visit the mermaid show, And as well felt like it would be great if the show happens in my country too, But who knows the show was in my city.*

*Well saw the Mermaid show, Well it was just for 10 minutes though!*

*And the craziness didn't leave me, as well as the eagerness of meeting her and talking a picture with her, So as soon as the show came to end, I dragged my family members and asked the staff where would the mermaid be and where no for taking a picture,*

*They replied to go to the 1st floor and you might find her there,*

*We went to the first floor and I was searching for the mermaid all over, but never happen to see her,*

*And I went in search of a mermaid and enquired many people, where would she be, they pointed to some random door and told me she might be coming out of that door, we were waiting for an hour next to the door, she never came.*

*Well, my disappointment level was too high, o was almost to the crying stage.*

*My father and brother went to the event management team and enquired about when will would you allow us to take a picture with the mermaid.*

*They said there is some timing for taking a picture and we had passed the timing and we pleased them and again asked mam was just waiting for the show and was waiting to take a picture with her, also said somehow arrange, please...*

*They just replied sorry we can't force her for taking a picture, With the full disappointment I stepped out of the marine kingdom, Without even having our lunch we went to visit the mermaid show, And a few hours went by.*

*And with that full disappointment, I didn't even have my lunch, later on, Well I even skipped my dinner just because of the disappointment of not taking a picture.*

*KA. PARINASRI*
*Theinnocentheart*

# Preface 2

## MOHAMMED NIYAZ

*(COMPILER)*

*Mohammed Niyaz hails from Mumbai - The City Of Dreams. He often loves to write poetries and short music video stories for his own youtube channel. Apart from this Mohammed is currently working on his upcoming anthologies, as well writing poetries since 2013. You can find him on facebook/mohammed niyaz as well on instagram @niyazsks.*

• • •

# (MYSTERY OF CREATIONS)

*Besides the world she's being considered with huge differences compared to humans.*
*Most of all the best creature ranked in the list of several regions.*
*Under the water, beneath the ground.*
*Always secure and subtle swimming surround.*
*Up above where most of the time rises till relations.*
*To the means of magical momentum hiding "mystery of creations".*

# Prologue

## SPECIAL NOTE BY KA. PARINASRI

*As KA. PARINASRI (owns the page named the innocentheart) is too much crazy on mermaids!*

*we all the co-authors from various parts of the world had decided to accompany her in her crazy mermaid antho by just giving out our imaginative write-up, especially for mermaids!*

*As soon as she (KA. PARINASRI) got the info about the mermaid show, she was too much existed and With her family members happened to visit the marine kingdom, She had visited it plenty of times whereas he family members as visiting it for the 1st time. They were as well eager to visit the show epically for the mermaid.*

*Because for the last few months they have been waiting for the mermaid show.*

*KA. PARINASRI still longs for talking at least a single selfie with her favourite mermaid Alexa.*

*We also hope that as per KA. PARINASRI, her dream/ wish of taking a selfie with her favourite mermaid dream comes true.*

# CO-AUTHORS ON BOARD

*1. SYEDAH HAFIZA RABIA IQBAL*

*2. YASMIN AMEEN*

*3. ROZY PAUL*

*4. RIYA RICHARD R L*

*5. DR. RITU GUPTA*

*6. VISHAKHA VERMA*

*7. JERLIN FLOWER S*

*8. BINOD DAWADI*

*9. MAID CORBIC*

*10. ANNE BENITA D*

# CO-AUTHORS ON BOARD

*11. RADHA RAMJIAWAN*

*12. S.REEJA*

*13. RANGEESH CHANDRASEKAR*

*14. W.A NEENA TAIMOORI*

CHAPTER I

# SYEDAH HAFIZA RABIA IQBAL

## "MESMERIZING SIGNOLA"

*Deep down island of love*
*Wine water and hazel dove*
*Crystal shadow with shiny edge*
*Wanna touch come to the ledge*
*I'm rare scattered light of hope*
*Without drinking I am a dope*
*Syedah*

CHAPTER II

# YASMIN AMEEN

## <u>DEAREST MERMAID!</u>

*My love for you is eternal,*
*I wish I could swim like you,*
*Roaming about in deep water would be so much fun!*
*Looking at your fishtail, i wish I had one too...*
*Dear Mermaid, i wish I could be you!*
*My love for you will never fade away...*

CHAPTER III

# ROZY PAUL

**QUOTE -**

*"Half fish half human alike beautiful creature of earth who is very pretty looks like queen and fond of water and living there as water baby."*

*Rozy Paul*

CHAPTER IV

# RIYA RICHARD R L

## MYTHICAL MERMAID

*Your eyes are Pearls unlike in oysters,*
*Your tail is Silky unlike Silk Moth*
*Your hair is Wavy unlike the Ocean waves*
*Your scales have golden Pixies unlike stars,*
*Your tears add Life, and your Smile adds Joy*
*You're Charming and Deceiving,*
*With the melodious voice of the Aqua,*
*Dancing in the Tides, Hiding in the Depth!*
*Riya Richard R L*

CHAPTER V

# DR. RITU GUPTA

## **ARIEL@MERMAID**

*Ariel, the Queen Of The Sea*
*You are UNIQUE, As beautiful can be...*
*Life Is Tough For You In The Waves*
*With Golden Locks And Fins Of Jade*
*Love the way you handle things*
*Bringing smile each time, to your kin!*
*@Ritu Gupta*

CHAPTER VI

# VISHAKHA VERMA

## MERMAID

*Dear Mermaid,*
*I am writing a short letter to you,*
*to tell you your value, your worth.*
*You know you are beautiful in your own way.*
*You are blessed with the natural beauty.*
*You are more than i can ever speak...*
*@Vishakha Verma*

CHAPTER VII

# JERLIN FLOWER S

## **MERMAID'S MELODY**

*Listening to the rhythm of the sea,*
*She closed her eyes...*
*Recollecting a stormy heart,*
*She fell hard on the rock bed.*
*The waves comforted her,*
*On a separate island.*
*Away from the hunting world.*
*In the world of her own!!!*
*-Jerlin Flower S*

CHAPTER VIII

# BINOD DAWADI

## MERMAID MY LOVER

*Mermaid you are my lover you stays in the sea,*
*You have half body of a fish half body of a human,*
*So from this characteristics,*
*You have also inner as well as outer beauty,*
*I like and love you will be be,*
*Mine your world and my world or life is a different you are mermaid,*
*As well as I am human I don't cares about world,*
*I love you so much.*
*©® Binod Dawadi*
*Nepal*

## QUOTES

*"Mermaid you are the gift of God made for me your uniqueness impressed me."*

*"Who is this half fish and half human she is a girl she is a beautiful mermaid I like her beautiful body."*

CHAPTER IX

# MAID CORBIC

## FOR MERMAIDS

*I share my wisdom of happiness*
*Mermaids are my deepest love*
*And I respect that surely*
*Due to my own visions*
*Spectrums of life is amazing*
*Mermaids is my happiness*
*And I want to have a dream*
*To be mermaid boy!*

CHAPTER X

# ANNE BENITA D

## HIDDEN ANGELS

*Beauty lies in the blessed creature of earth,*
*Half human, half fish, the hidden angels of ocean;*
*Benevolence is the heart, boons is the wish,*
*A free bird in the depth of the hidden seas.*
*The stars of the ocean are in the tales and the dream,*
*Truth is hidden in the pen and the books;*
*Glory and grace is the privilege of the them,*
*Let the hidden angels come to the world soon.*

*By*
*Anne Benita D*

CHAPTER XI

# RADHA RAMJIAWAN

## **"I SAW A BIG GOLDEN TAIL**

## **MOVING IN THE MIDDLE OF THE SEA"**

*I saw a big golden tail moving in the middle of the sea.*
*So I came rowing, more closer at the middle of the sea.*
*Full of amazement, I saw in the water a beautiful female.*
*Slapped twice on my face, but still I saw a female.*
*When I did take a good look, I saw it was a mermaid.*
*I was admiring the beautiful mermaid.*
*Then suddenly the mermaid saw me and startled, she went in the depth for forever.*
*Co - author: Radha Ramjiawan*
*Insta@radharamjiawan*

CHAPTER XII

# S.REEJA

## ANGEL IN MYSELF

*Your are the sigh of hope*
*It gives us the rope of scope*
*You are the Angel of the ocean*
*Sunk all my feelings and emotion*
*Each personality has a character of mermaid*
*Overcoming all the resentment is the pride*
*Bring out the special character from your heart*
*It will sketch your life with art*
*S.Reeja*

CHAPTER XIII

# RANGEESH CHANDRASEKAR

## SWIMMING IN THE

## WHIRLPOOL OF EMOTIONS

*That windy night, laid awestruck on the bed with pillows as the mates,*
*And No one! No one! To accompany the isolated skeleton;*
*Emotions dawned upon the emerging arena of thoughts:*
*Making me dive into the long ocean of sensations!*
*Those tides of black water in the sea of sorrow;*
*Me twirling amongst the wavy taunts like a swimming butterfly!*
*Those fishes of grief and lichens of broken friendship;*
*Accompanied me through my journey amidst the dark sea!*
*Long and Long away, A ship of hopes seemed sailing,*
*Waving at it, I failed and kept swimming through the dusk!*
*Typhoon of strife arrived at my threshold- shattering all my might,*
*Yet! Those dolphins of strength, enhanced my zeal to dawn.....*
*I swam, swam and swam.... Long through the channel,*
*Met with the mermaid, the abode of beauty and adore!*
*The figure befriended me, ultimately befooling my trust;*
*Yet! Those dolphins of strength, enhanced my zeal to dawn.....*

*O There! I reached an island of ecstasy, and greenery as it's sole inhabitant;*
*The splendid trees with coconuts hanging down were the rays of desires!*
*I made the hut with twigs and branches lying at the shore,*
*And lived amongst the tides and the sandy beaches!*
*That swimming through the dusky ocean,*
*Outstretched me to the shore of euphoria, reshaping my destiny!*

*Rangeesh Chandrasekar*
*Insta: rangeeshc_1410*

CHAPTER XIV

# W.A NEENA TAIMOORI

## NAUTICAL BEAUTY

*Flip flapping her beautiful tail*
*A fish I saw in the moonlit trail*
*Primarily I neglected- as I daily saw fishes*
*That is not unusual for a fisher*
*Black, silver, red or blue*
*I have seen them in every hue*
*But when it shimmer*
*I could not waiver*
*I rowed the yacht*
*Near the rock*
*She peers at me*
*And in the brine, she fades*
*That was the last juncture I witnessed beauty*
*I wait for her to date— she never came near or passed by*
*— NeenaT ©*
*0606022*

Printed by Libri Plureos GmbH in Hamburg,
Germany